Around the World!

adapted by Suzanne D. Nimm
based on the original teleplay written by Valerie Walsh
illustrated by Ron Zalme

SCHOLASTIC INC.
New York Toronto London Auckland Sydney
Mexico City New Delhi Hong Kong Buenos Aires

ISBN-13: 978-0-439-87049-8
ISBN-10: 0-439-87049-6

12 11 10 9 8 7 6 5 4 3 2 1   7 8 9 10 11/0

Printed in the U.S.A.

First Scholastic printing, February 2007

Hi! I am  .

DORA

Today is Friendship Day!

 swiped all

SWIPER

of the friendship  !

BRACELETS

Now we have to return them

to our friends around the !

WORLD

Will you help us

deliver the friendship  ?
BRACELETS

Great!

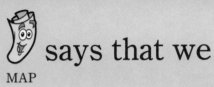 says that we

MAP

have to bring

BRACELETS

to our friends

at the in France,

TOWER

the ![mountain] in Tanzania,
MOUNTAIN

the ![palace] in Russia,
PALACE

and the Great ![wall] of China.
WALL

We are in France!

Where is the Eiffel ?

TOWER

We have to follow

the road with  DIAMONDS

to get to the Eiffel ▲. TOWER

Do you see ◆ ?
DIAMONDS

Fifi the  will try

SKUNK

to swipe our !

BRACELETS

Do you see a ?

SKUNK

Oh, no! Say "No swiping!"

Thanks for stopping the !
SKUNK

Now our friends in France

can get friendship .
BRACELETS

We are in Tanzania!

This 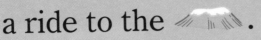 is giving us

ELEPHANT

a ride to the .

MOUNTAIN

Look! I see a and a .

ZEBRA   LION

Uh-oh! Sami the
HYENA
will try

to swipe the friendship .
BRACELETS

If you see a , say
HYENA

"No swiping!"

All of our friends

are so happy

to get their  !
BRACELETS

Next we have to ride

in a 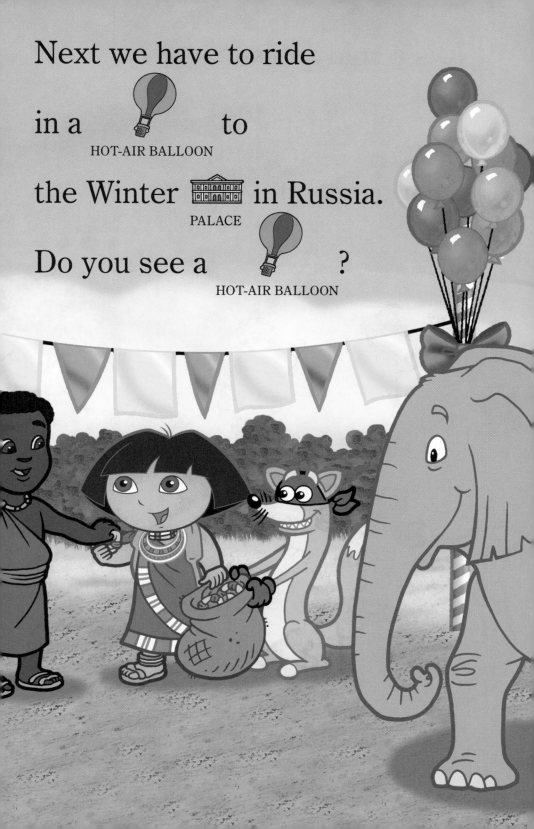 to

HOT-AIR BALLOON

the Winter 🏛 in Russia.

PALACE

Do you see a 🎈 ?

HOT-AIR BALLOON

It is a cold and snowy day.

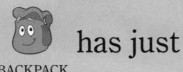 has just

what we need!

Do you see a  COAT , MITTENS ,

a HAT , and SKIS ?

Now we can give out

friendship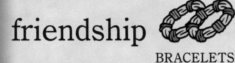
BRACELETS

to our friends in Russia.

Look! One is different
SNOWMAN

from the other .
SNOWMAN

Wait—it is Fomkah the

sneaky !

BEAR

Fomkah wants to swipe

the friendship .

BRACELETS

Say "No swiping!"

Now we can give out

the 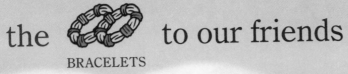 to our friends
BRACELETS

at the Great of China.
WALL

Ying-Ying the

will try to swipe the .

Say "No swiping!"

Look! There is one  left.

BRACELET

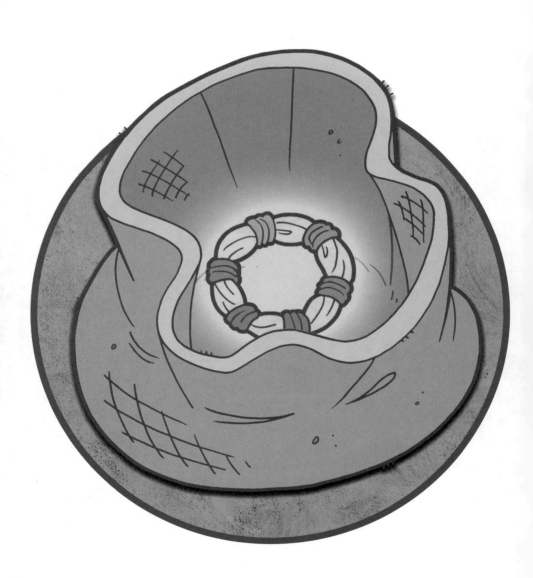

It is a friendship for !

BRACELET   SWIPER

Now everyone has a  .

BRACELET

Thank you for helping us

deliver the friendship
BRACELETS

to all our friends around the !
WORLD

Happy Friendship Day!